Cocoloco Joins the choir

By Luis Velázquez
Illustrated by Jason Velázquez

Cocoloco Joins The Choir

© 2020 by Luis Velázquez

Illustrated by Jason Velázquez

Printed in the United States of America.

ISBN-13: 978-1-7353045-2-1

Three Arrows

PUBLISHING

Long Island, New York

At the time of this publication,

Rev. Luis Velazquez is an Ordained Minister with the Assemblies of God and is the District Director for the Royal Rangers Ministry in the Spanish Eastern District. He is also a member of the National Royal Rangers Ministry Executive Council holding the position of Eastern U.S. Hispanic Representative.

His passion has always been to minister to children and youth wherever the Lord has placed him. This passion has allowed him and his wife Jasmin, to work as Children's Pastors, Youth Pastors and Education Ministers in congregations in Brooklyn and Long Island N.Y. Currently they are Associate Ministers at Calvary International Church in Brooklyn, N.Y. He is also the founder of A Time to Laugh Puppet and Clown ministry which trains young people in the use of puppets to minister to young children. His books are a retelling of some of the stories he has used to bring God's word to the hearts of children and youth everywhere.

After 32 years he retired from teaching in the NYC Public School System. He is married to Jasmin and has been blessed with two young ladies, Jasmin Crystal and Ruth Elizabeth.

Cocoloco was excited! He had been waiting for this day a long time. As he lay in his bed, with the covers up to his neck, he thought of all the things that were going to happen today. If only Ava would get here.

WOOSH!

Then he heard the words he was waiting for: "Ava is here," his mother called.

ZIP!

Cocoloco jumped out of his bed, already dressed and ready to go!

DING DONG

You see, he woke up early and prepared himself for the day. He ran to the door, and there he saw his good friend, Ava.

Ava was the one who told Cocoloco about the opportunity to join the church choir. She let him know that today was the day that he would have the chance to audition for the children's choir at their church. Cocoloco had seen the choir perform, and he knew that he could sing just as good as some of the kids in that choir. In fact, he knew that he was a better singer than all of them.

"Are you ready, Cocoloco?" Ava asked.
"I am super ready!" he answered.
Off they went to church.

Cocoloco and Ava arrived at the church. As they entered, they could see the choir members taking their seats in the pews. Cocoloco recognized some of them. Some were in his Sunday School class, some he had seen in children's church, and the other members he didn't know personally.

The person in charge of the choir is called Hermana (or Sister) Pirulina. Cocoloco always thought she was a good choir director. She also led the adult choir.

Hna. Pirulina was asking all the members of the choir to sit down and listen. She opened up a Bible and began to read. She read from the Book of Psalms, chapter 100, verse 2.

"Worship the Lord with gladness; come before him with joyful songs."

Then she said, "Choir members, we must remember the primary reason we sing is to worship our Lord. He loves us and we love Him. With our songs, we can thank Him, we can praise Him, and we can ask for His help. Another part of worship is prayer. With our words, we can speak to God and let Him know how we feel. He is always ready to listen if we want to talk. When we sing and pray, it's not about how well we can sing or what fancy words we use to pray. It's about knowing who God is and His place in our hearts. So, before we begin our practice, let us pray."

Everyone bowed their heads and closed their eyes as Hna. Pirulina prayed.

"Thank You, Lord, for this day. Thank You for the opportunity to practice with all these wonderful children. We lift our voices to You in worship because You loved us first. We also thank You for Cocoloco, who came today to audition for the choir. In Jesus' name, amen."

Wow! He was surprised that she knew his name, and she prayed for him! Now, Cocoloco was super excited! He knew that when he sang, he would surprise everyone with his voice!

Hna. Pirulina was getting ready for practice. She separated the choir members by voices. There were the sopranos, then the altos stood together, the tenors were next, and then some were in a group called baritone. Cocoloco had never realized there were so many different voices.

Then, they began to sing. It was beautiful! They sang and sang and sang and sang. They would stop, then start again, then stop again. Ava had a solo, and she sang beautifully. Although it sounded good, Cocoloco couldn't wait for the choir practice to end so that he could show them what real singing was like. If only they would finish. Finally, the director called for a break. Hna. Pirulina and Ava walked over to Cocoloco.

Ava asked, "Are you ready for your audition, Cocoloco?"

"I am super ready!" Cocoloco answered.

The three of them walked over to a little room for the audition. Hna Pirulina said, "Thank you, Cocoloco, and welcome to the choir auditions. Do you know in which voice you sing? Are you a soprano or alto? Maybe you're a tenor or maybe even a baritone?"

"Is there a voice called spectacular, or super, or even super spectacular? That's the voice I have! I don't know about all those others," he said.

Hna. Pirulina looked at him funny, then she announced, "OK, Cocoloco, you can sing any song you like whenever you are ready."

"Good luck, Cocoloco!" Ava said.

Cocoloco prepared himself. He thought of all the times he had practiced this song. He sang in the shower, on his way to school, while he was playing, and just before going to bed. They were going to love his voice! Cocoloco cleared his voice. "Ahem, ahem!" He began to sing..."Ahmaaaazing grace," then suddenly, his voice cracked!

Cocoloco was embarrassed! This had never happened to him before.

"Please try again," Hna. Pirulina said.

He sang again, and his voice cracked again! Cocoloco saw the disappointment in their faces. They spoke in whispers to each other and then turned to him.

Hna. Pirulina spoke first. "I'm sorry, Cocoloco, but you won't be able to be a part of the choir at this time. You can try again when we have tryouts later in the year."

Ava spoke next. "I'm really sorry, Cocoloco."

Hna. Pirulina and Ava walked out of the room and left the door open.

Cocoloco stayed in the room. How could he go out and face them? The choir would know that he failed. They were probably laughing at him right now. He became sad, then he became angry! He knew he could sing, he knew he could do better. Then he remembered what Hna. Pirulina said. Worship was about singing and praying to God. It wasn't about how well you sang or singing better than someone else. Cocoloco knew what he had to do. In the room all by himself, Cocoloco bowed his head and closed his eyes and began to pray.

"Hi God, it's me, Cocoloco. I hope You are listening. I am sorry. I wanted to show everyone how well I sing. I wanted everyone to know that I had a great voice, but I forgot the reason we sing. It's to worship You. So, even though I didn't sing very well and I can't join the choir, I will try my best next time. Next time, I will sing for You because I know You love me, and I want to show You that I love You. One more thing, since no one is listening, can I sing a song to You, Jesus?" Cocoloco prepared himself to sing. He forgot about everything else, and in a soft, quiet voice, he started singing a song he would hear his mother sing at home.

"I love You, Lord; You make me strong.
With all my heart, I praise You, and all hurt is gone.
You're my rock, my shield, and You're forever near.
Gone is my doubt, all my pain, and all my fear."

He continued to sing and didn't notice when Ana, Pirulina and Ava entered the room. When he finished, he turned around and saw them in the room, and also saw that the whole choir was looking in at him through the open door.

"I'm sorry, Hna. Pirulina!" he said. "I was just singing to Jesus, and I didn't mean to interrupt your practice. I'll leave now."

"Are you kidding, Cocoloco?" she said, "You sang beautifully! I could tell that you were singing from the heart. That is what worship is all about. I think we can use another true worshiper in our choir. Even if we have to spend some time teaching your voice not to crack. What do you think, Ava?"

"I think you are correct, Hna. Pirulina!" she said

Hna. Pirulina turned to the choir and asked, "What do you think, choir?"
They all cheered!
"So, Cocoloco, it seems we have some work to do. When you are ready, come and join our practice!"

As Ava and Hna. Pirulina walked out of the room, Cocoloco could scream. Instead, he bowed his head and they all could hear him pray:

"Thank You, God. I will never forget what I have learned here today. I will sing for You with all my heart to please You and no one else! Now, please help me, as we practice. All honor and glory is Yours. In Jesus' name, I pray! Amen!

As he left the room, you could hear him say, "I'm going to join the choir! I'm going to join the choir! I'm going to join the choir!"

That day, Cocoloco joined the children's choir.

The choir was never the same!

But that's another story!

CPSIA information can be obtained
at www.ICGtesting.com
Printed in the USA
LVHW010852121120
671500LV00005B/221